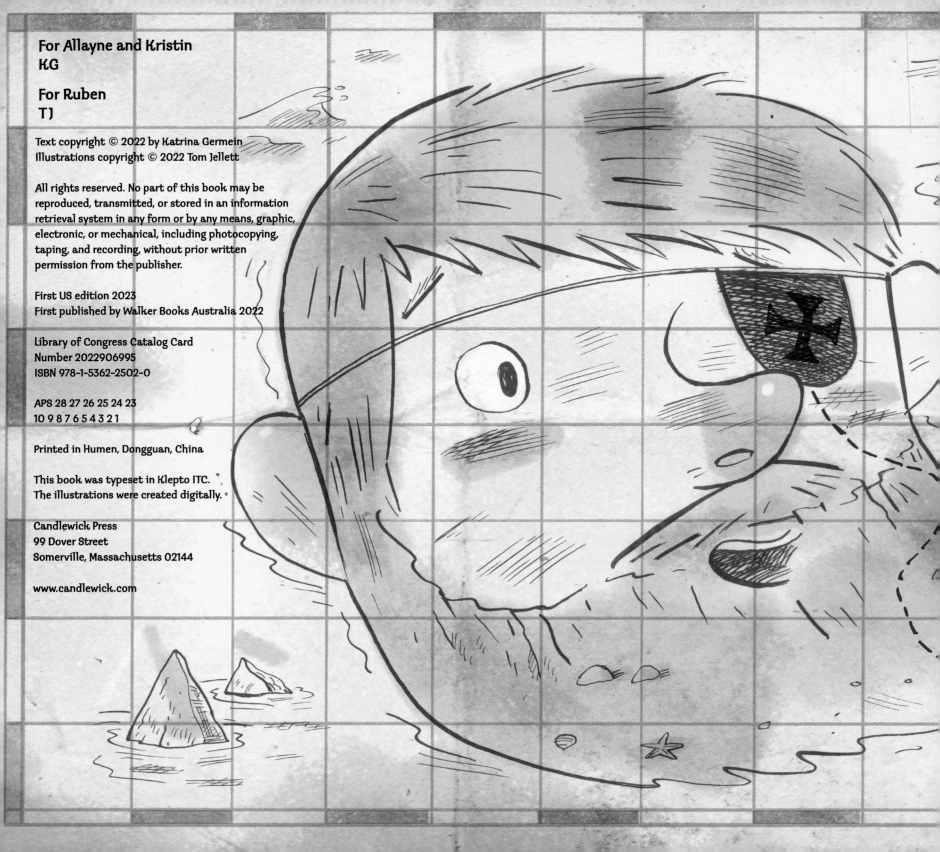

For Allayne and Kristin
KG

For Ruben
TJ

Text copyright © 2022 by Katrina Germein
Illustrations copyright © 2022 Tom Jellett

First US edition 2023
First published by Walker Books Australia 2022

Library of Congress Catalog Card
Number 2022906995
ISBN 978-1-5362-2502-0

APS 28 27 26 25 24 23
10 9 8 7 6 5 4 3 2 1

Printed in Humen, Dongguan, China

This book was typeset in Klepto ITC.
The illustrations were created digitally.

Candlewick Press
99 Dover Street
Somerville, Massachusetts 02144

www.candlewick.com

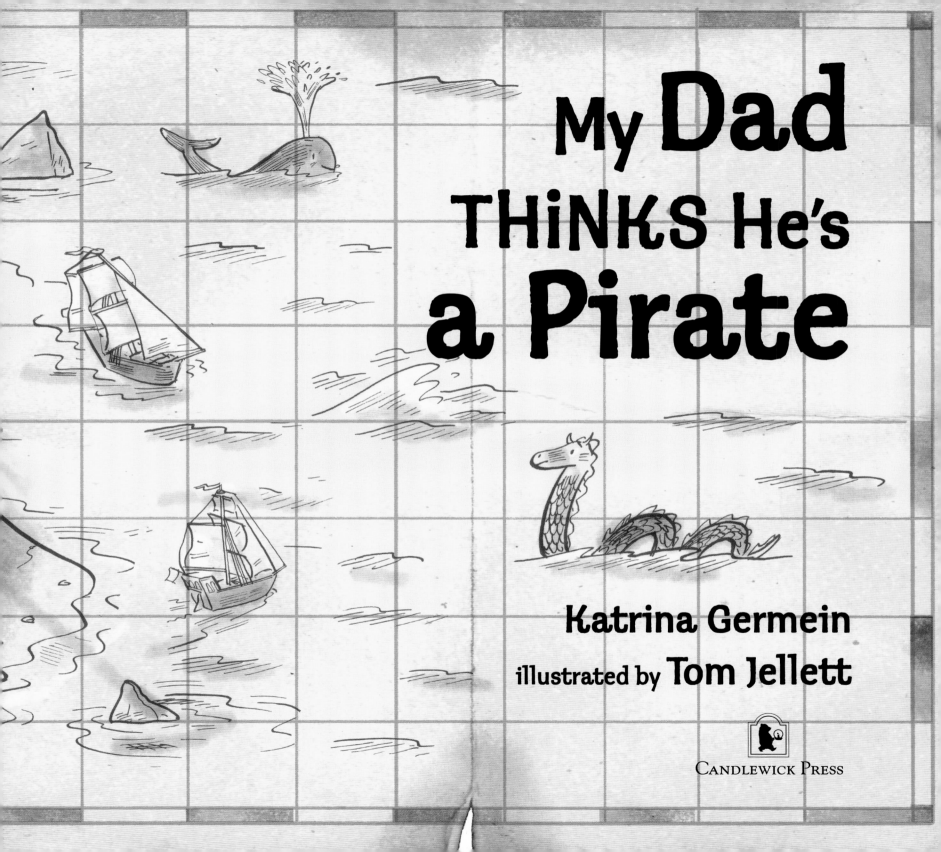

My Dad THINKS He's a Pirate

Katrina Germein

illustrated by Tom Jellett

CANDLEWICK PRESS

My dad thinks he's funny.

"Knock, knock," says Dad.

"Who's there?" I say.

"Turner," says Dad.

"Turner who?" I say.

"Turner round, there's a pirate behind you!"

My dad thinks he's a pirate.

"Come on, me heartie. We've treasure to find."

"Aye, aye," I reply.

"Just one aye," says Dad, and points to his patch.
"Here's our ship.
I bought it on sail."

"Let's go!" I say.

"Hold on, scallywag," Dad replies.
"We need this hat to go on ahead."

My dad thinks he's a pirate.

"Hello, ocean," calls Dad.
"Long time no sea."

"This is fun," I say.

"Shore is," says Dad.
"The sea is so friendly.
It always waves."

My dad thinks he's a pirate.

Dad calls out . . .

"Pass me the telescope.
It makes me look better!

Watch out for shellfish.
They make me crabby.

Watch out for squid.
They're always well armed."

My dad thinks he's a pirate.

"Let's eat on the beach,"
Dad declares, "**because of all the sand-which-is there.**

My dad thinks he's a pirate.

"We should carry our swords," Dad remarks.

"Why?" I ask.

"Because swords can't walk!"

It sure is a windy day!"

My dad thinks he's a pirate.

_X_ marks the spot!
We need a shovel.

"Heave ho!" says Dad. **"I'm digging this!"**

"I'm getting tired, Dad," I say.

"Dig deep!" he says.
"The pirate life is full of hard-ships."

Hooray!
The buried treasure chest!

"Gold rocks!" says Dad. "But you're my favorite treasure."

My dad thinks he's a pirate.

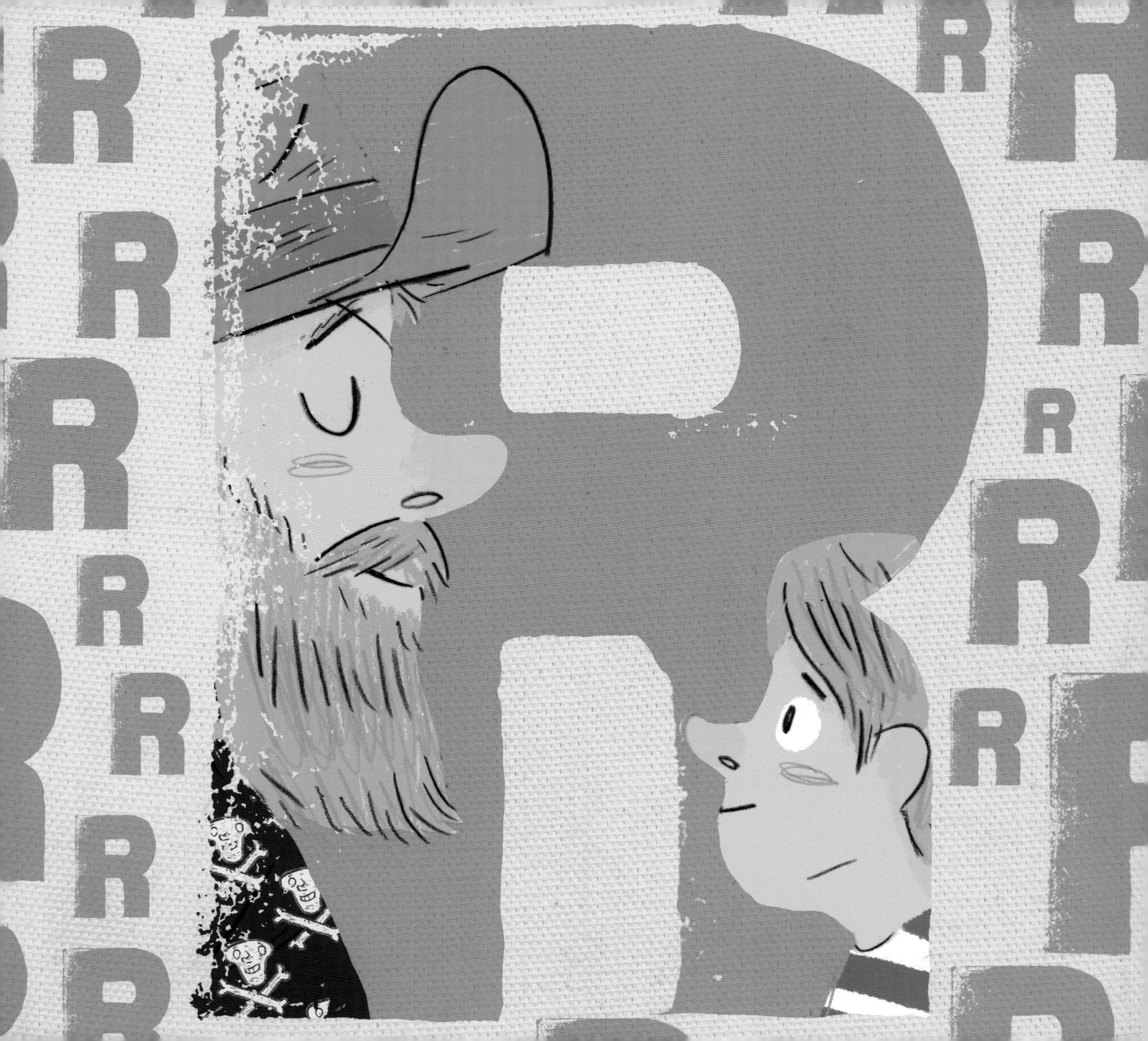

"Do you know why pirates are funny?" asks Dad.

"Why?" I say.

"Well," says Dad, **"because they arrrrr."**

My dad thinks he's a pirate.

By hook or by crook, you've read the whole book.